Alphapoetical Soup

An A-Z Collection of Poetic Forms

written by Dorie Deats

illustrated by Joanna Pasek

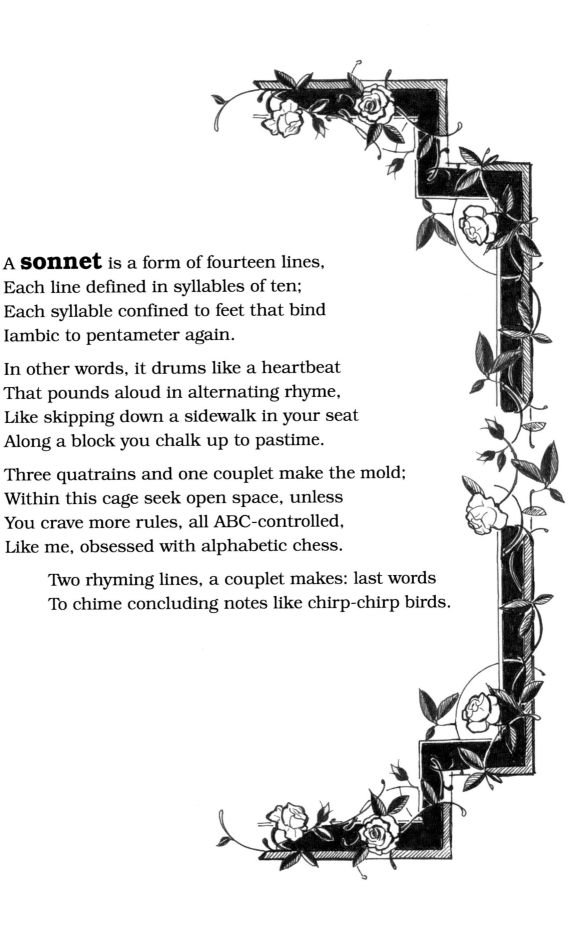

A **sonnet** is a form of fourteen lines,
Each line defined in syllables of ten;
Each syllable confined to feet that bind
Iambic to pentameter again.

In other words, it drums like a heartbeat
That pounds aloud in alternating rhyme,
Like skipping down a sidewalk in your seat
Along a block you chalk up to pastime.

Three quatrains and one couplet make the mold;
Within this cage seek open space, unless
You crave more rules, all ABC-controlled,
Like me, obsessed with alphabetic chess.

    Two rhyming lines, a couplet makes: last words
    To chime concluding notes like chirp-chirp birds.

Aurora all adorned in autumn leaves
    Ascends an apple tree, sunset aglow,
And in between the branches quickly weaves
A hammock web; a bed for laying low.

Aurora all alone when moon is high
Awakes to contemplate the midnight view
Alit with stars that span the endless sky
And glitter like the grass when met with dew.

Aurora all abloom in morning light
Arises alongside the early birds
And with them wings a hymn of taking flight
And rides their wind-worn path of sing-song words.

    Aurora, fiery fairy of Fall air,
    Blends greens with reds in golden threads trees wear.

eholding ballerinas on a boat,
Babette becomes bad-tempered and begins
Bewailing like a princess in a moat,
Bemoaning that no slippers fit her fins.

Believing she's a human badly cursed,
Babette begrudges bodies that have legs,
Belittles them, begetting bloody thirst
to tip their ship and drown them in the dregs.

But when a dancing doll does flailing fall
Beneath the barge, each limb a useless stick,
Babette, the fairest swimmer of them all,
Besets the girl and coaches her to kick.

Babette unbinds her blindfold of ill wills,
Confirmed now that deep breathing calls for gills.

Clarice Clairvoyant, according to her cats,
   Campaigns to lead a Calico Brigade.
Conjectured an "eccentric crone" and "bats"—
Clarice cares not, just wants her own parade.

Colliding with the City Council's vote,
Clarice commits to canvassing the town,
Commanding crowds from high upon her float,
Crusading to claw all conventions down.

Clarice calls for a Carnival where cats
Can claim their rightful crowns as Queen or King,
Can clown around alongside country rats,
Can catch or throw all bling-things put to string.

   Clarice's coup d'état, live on channel 9,
   Declares her Mardi Gras' deity feline.

Delilah is a duchess who delights
    Demonstrably in decorated cakes.
Daydreaming doughnuts dipped in chocolate nights,
Delilah plays "pâtissière," then wakes.

Delilah, quite the critic of desserts,
Defines decorum of the palate arts,
Demanding masses standing at her skirts
Deep bow to highbrow musings on puff tarts.

Delilah, draped in layers doberge-like,
Dons hats to fatly match her derrière,
Descending on a bakery on strike,
Delilah simply seeks a mousse èclair.

    Dumbfounded by a riot's dearth of sweets,
    Estranged, she deigns to stroll the fruitful streets.

Enigma, Elven-born, enchants an egg,
Enwraps it in an old elixir spell
Encases it in gold—out kicks a leg,
Erupting the rich jewel-encrusted shell.

Excited for escape, the hatchling peeps,
Emerging eagle-headed, lion-tailed.
Enigma gasps enraptured, kneeling, weeps,
Encountering a griffin babe unveiled.

Expressive is this birdling beast called "Eep,"
Emitting sounds exclaiming endless glee,
Exhibiting instincts to fly and leap,
Elated by existence, new and free.

Embracing Eep, Enigma's heart is glad;
Forsaking sleep, he finds he is a dad.

Cinquain

Cinquain:

Five line poem

Centered in this order—

Two, four, six, eight, two syllables

Per line.

L aelyn:

Fair forest sprite,

Fern-fringed and feather-crowned,

Fell for a frog, fond at first sight,

Gem-bound.

Gawain:

Good knight, gone pale,

Green-gilled with fate to face;

Golden as grail, his word won't fail

His Grace.

Haunting

Hellen Lee hoots,

Howling her horrid laugh;

Holding high her ghost axe, hacks fruits

In half.

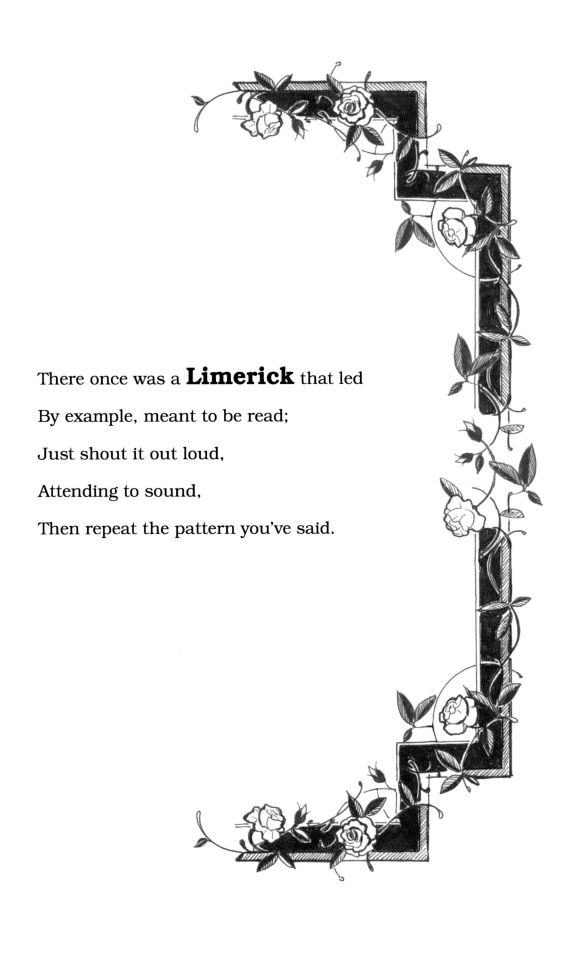

There once was a **Limerick** that led

By example, meant to be read;

Just shout it out loud,

Attending to sound,

Then repeat the pattern you've said.

Icknor, an insurance troll

Inflates his "bridge safety" toll,

Insisting you cross,

Investing your loss,

Just selling his ill-fated soul.

Jester John played love songs, went too far,

Jamming odes on his olden guitar;

Jelly-hearted, the queen

Jumped and screamed like a tween,

Keen on courting her clown-turned-rock-star.

Kate, runaway kangaroo model

Known far for her catwalking waddle,

Kicked high her cramped knees,

Kite-like as you please,

Leaping from the staged cage of her dawdle.

Lenora, a leprechaun lass,

Leaned into a pot sprouting grass;

Looking for gold

Lying untold,

Mining seeds from weeds grown in brass.

arinda, ice mermaid from Mars,

Met a Venus cowboy called Lars.

Match-made through Space-Site,

Moving lightyears in flight,

Now they date at Earth's midway bars.

None other than Norman the gnome

Narrated tomes at Nan's nursing home;

No nursery rhyme pillars

Nor crime novel thrillers...

Only plant guides for gardeners who roam.

Once rumored to have owl eyes,

Oft thought a warlock in disguise;

Old man he appears,

Outshining the years,

Pete sleeps on sidewalks to see skies.

oinsettia, opossum princess,

Posing purple with blossomed headdress,

Prancing all paws about,

Pointing out a proud snout,

Quite lampooned her queen mother's success.

A **Haiku**'s lifespan

Flashes by five-seven-five

Fast flaps of a fan.

Quicksilver monster

Quakes awake quiet water,

Raining up moonlight.

avenous rag dolls

Ransack refrigerators

Searching for stuffing.

Serpent girl, shale-scaled,

Sheds her tall tail, shuffling off

This mortal coil.

Tess, the Grand High Tree,

Takes tea with a bird named Bea

Under summer leaves.

Unicorn storm clouds

Uprise against pollution

Voicing their thunder.

ials of vapors

Ventilate vaulted venues

Where vampires waltz.

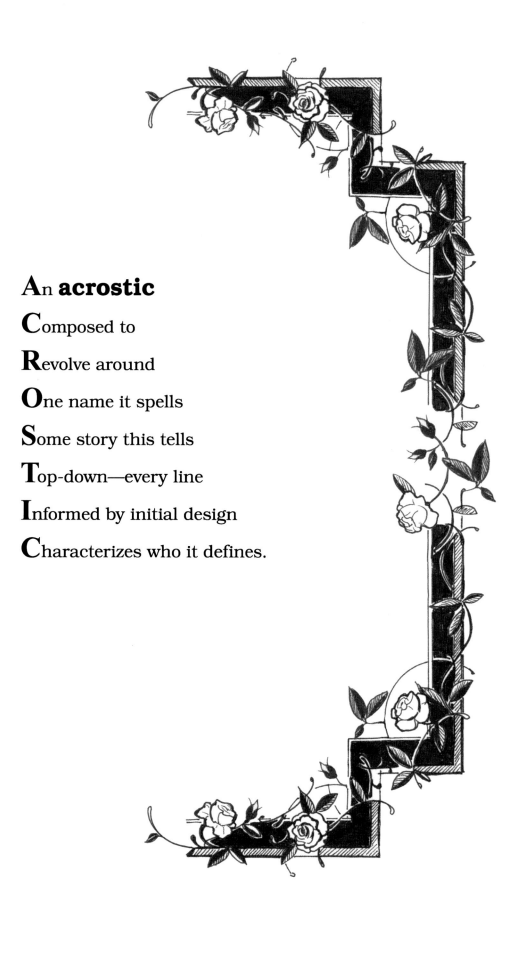

An **acrostic**

Composed to

Revolve around

One name it spells

Some story this tells

Top-down—every line

Informed by initial design

Characterizes who it defines.

Wearing a weathervane wedged in her hat,

Intercepting radio waves, she checks

News of Witch World Convention, where sat

Only winners, at their windswept apex,

Nominated by her worst rival that

Adored her once—wicked hex-worthy Ex!

E**X**plorer of ground,

Ex**A**miner of stone,

Exca**V**ated a mound,

Its ex**I**stence unknown—

Th**E** T-Rex had found

Yo**R**e-times' human bone!

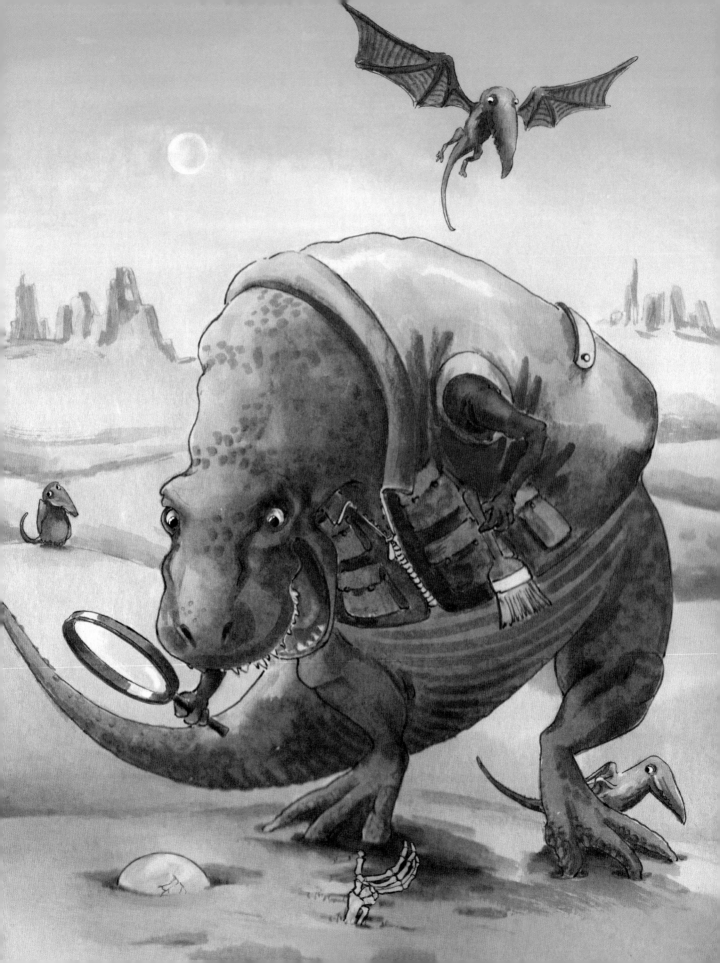

Yin-yangs arrayed in his yarn-yellow locks,

A yogi, a hippie, a man made of breeze,

Rented a yurt yielding crystals and rocks,

Retreating from yearning urban unease

Of yesterday's deep meditation talks,

Wise-weary and yawning, seeking some Zzzs...

Zeroing in on her most zealous quest,

Experimenting with zircon and zinc,

Lab-mad, she zigzags through each zany test,

Distilling stars, jarring zodiac ink,

Astral-writing proofs with quizzical zest.

For my incurably verbal mother—

Only you, who taught me my ABCs

Rejoice in my word play like no other,

Making endless time for my 123s

Of syllable-count, my metric stutter—

Marion Deats—thanks for my Do-Re-Meees!